Shadow Trappers

The Fictional Autobiography of Katerina Chen

By X. Ellington

Introduction

Schizophrenia is not a choice. When the right circumstances present themselves, a sudden surge of psycho paranoia takes control of your world and thoughts, and there is not much you can do.

In hindsight, my choice to lose things—memories, lovers, random inanimate objects, routes to destinations, and keys—led me on a quest to try and find myself again.

I am Katerina Chen, and this is my story—the story of fear, anguish, injustice, and a desperate, fruitless quest to find what was lost. The story I'm about to share with you is all true, and is based on my condition, known as schizophrenia. I hope you enjoy my autobiographical tale, Shadow Trappers.

Hello, I'm Katerina.

Chapter One: The Accident

One September, I remember, I was in a car accident that lasted three weeks. Not really, but in my mind, it was at least that long. It was an endless 3-week battle of car accident nightmares.

Back then, I drove a red, fitness-explosion, super-hydro van; at least that's what I called it. I would commute to work, where I was a cosmetics saleswoman. Sometimes I would use my super-hydro van to deliver flowers around the holidays for extra cash. It was easy to find things I needed back then: money, love, delicious meals, and interesting client-related banter. I never would have imagined myself a victim, but my beloved, super-hydro van had failed me. I would no longer be able to live the life I once had. I was someone who enjoyed my life as well as my independence. Lying helpless in a hospital bed with my mind in disarray, I knew my dreams were over. I will never forget that feeling.

And I will always remember the first nightmare because it was so vivid and real. I recall the accident, of course, but in my schizophrenic nightmare, the car accident featured Shadow Orbs of ancient myth and legend; these were my Shadow Orbs. I also saw a vision of myself in an out-of-body kind of way, as if I were viewing the whole experience from a third-person point of view. I could see everything: the accident, the Shadow Orbs, and my extreme pain. It was so awful.

After my accident, I was a mess. I could not talk or walk for about 9 months. I had suffered multiple concussions, and none of it was even my fault. A drunk driver in a semi caused my beloved, super-hydro van to crash. He didn't make it, and I was hanging on by a thread!

Often, I would just lay in my hospital bed, watching myself from the ceiling. During those nine months, I remember very little, except that I was not in my body but rather watching over myself as if I were watching a movie starring me!

Of course, I couldn't move. It was not an exciting movie, let me tell you. Every so often, a nurse or doctor would come into the picture, and they were great. They never looked at me watching us from the ceiling—such fine acting!

Furthermore, the vague recollection of my memories as I lie in and out of consciousness seemed to coincide with the memories of another past life—one that was not my own. I didn't know who I was or what my life had been. This other person's memories filled in the gaps, and it was hard to picture anything as reality after that. Even after I began speaking and then walking again, the reality in my head was not the truth—it was not me; it was a movie. A past life as an actress filled in all the memories I'd lost from the accident. Someone who at one time had great promise and potential, but suddenly and quite violently, it was all ripped away from her. I also remember the Shadow Orbs.

Shadow Orbs of all different shapes and sizes would creep sometimes in the night, surrounding me as I lay in my hospital bed. I could see them from the ceiling—like I said, I was in a movie. I couldn't move, so I couldn't do anything about it. Oh, the horror in my mind! I was watching this happen—to me! It was my movie, but I was never sure if I would make it or who exactly was directing it. I remember thinking sometimes that if I concentrated on remembering my past life—even if it wasn't my life I was remembering—then the Shadow Orbs would not take me away. I still remember the horror, the fear, and the memory of witnessing my own meaningless life struggling to survive from my imaginary ceiling view.

The Shadow Orbs at the Hospital

Chapter Two: Carol

Carol was my best friend after I left the hospital. She would always tell me that if I kept speaking, then the Shadow Orbs would stop visiting me... for a time. Carol knew an exemplary amount of information about the Shadow Orbs and taught me how to deal with them when they returned. For a while, it seemed that I was unstoppable with Carol around. Unfortunately, even with Carol, my false memories persisted.

I wanted to get a pension for the past acting work I had done. My false memories informed me that I was eligible for a pension because my accident prevented me from working. I was owed this money plus back pay, and I was determined to find an attorney who would take my case. In those years, I called many different people, all of whom seemed to elude me. I could never get a straight answer. Even the attorneys who agreed to listen to my story never called me again, and they never returned my follow-up calls. I was growing discouraged. It had been years since the accident. Perhaps I had made a mistake. Carol never approved of me seeking money I was owed.

"Who cares about acting money? If you are going to survive, you have to start thinking about the present or the Shadow Orbs will scoop you up," explained Carol.

According to Carol, this idea of old money from a past life was drawing the ire of the Shadow Orbs. Carol warned me. She said if I pursued this money I was allegedly owed in my mind, then the Shadow Orbs would get greedy and try to steal me away before I could have a chance at a new life with my pension money—money that was not actually mine. As Carol once said, the Shadow Orbs wanted my life for themselves.

"Only through your life can the Shadow Orbs obtain true form," said Carol. "You are special to them, Katerina, especially when your mind wanders like it does."

I was special because I survived—or rather, my body survived. The events depicted in the movie I was watching made me realize that my mind and spirit were devoid of reality. What was once real was lost. What I had now was ever-changing. Exciting times, if you forget about the fear and anguish I would consistently feel. Now was my chance to let go of these false memories that I thought would somehow free me. How could money free the mind and soul, anyway?

I had to listen to Carol, the one person I could count on going forward. Carol was someone I trusted, so I believed everything she said. There were no lies between us. She was my best friend.

Carol

Chapter Three: Calamity Sam

"There's no way to tell if a dog is sick, unless he's done ralphin' in plain sight." - Calamity Sam

Calamity Sam had it made. Sam, like me, received his disability money on the 3rd of every month! The first week of money allowed us to hang out in the forest and have fun. We would drink, start fires, take pills, and tell stories. I would tell him stories of my made-up acting days, while he would tell me stories about different animal encounters, usually involving dogs and raccoons. Carol and I would laugh at Sam's stories, and we would always have a good time.

The name, Calamity, came from something he would occasionally allude to about his past, although never directly. It is something he would talk about, not just to me but literally everyone, called the Calamity Proposition.

Basically, it was a plan about how he could really shake things up by convincing everyone that he was Jesus Christ. He was often oblivious to the offense he would create in some people. Everyone called him Calamity Sam because of the stir he would cause when he said things like this. None of us were exactly sure why Sam believed this, but something happened to him in the past.

I asked him about the Jesus thing and why he believed what he did. Usually, his reply was that it was just something he had to do.

But there was one time when Sam's reply was more cryptic and revealing. He mentioned a past animal friend, a truck accident, and simply stated that he needed to atone; he had to make a sacrifice.

In retrospect, it is clear to me that Sam had done something so horrible, at least in his mind, that he repressed the past event and tried to replace it with a pathway to redemption. In a sense, we had it all figured out, but for Sam, that potential pathway to redemption crumbled before he could reach the finish line. I understood Sam—he blamed himself for the death of his animal friend, and that was all.

Later, Carol and I would tell Sam it's not his fault, and for a while we could literally see the guilt melt away from him. The Jesus thing would go away for a while, too. We could thank God for that, or maybe I should have thanked Carol. Carol understood Sam even better than I did.

Carol would say this about Calamity Sam:

"You know Katerina? There is a good chance that he could be right, and wouldn't it be great if our Lord and Savior were hanging out with us, getting high with us, in the forest every night?"

It was a cool fantasy that I humored and would do so forever, even if it meant lying to myself a little.

"Hey Calamity!" I would say, "Are we in revelation yet?"

And Sam would always reply,

"Revelation!?! Revelation is old news! I am here. I know the way. I am the way. I just need y'all to follow me. She-it!"

And my reply was always,

"We're following, we're following!"

One time, Calamity Sam was in a heated debate that was normally avoided by an assortment of different types of mood elevators he would take whenever we were at the bar so he could stay cool. The heated discussion was with a man about the same age as Sam. Sam was in his forties.

It began with Sam's comment, "You're right, I do know."

Evidently, the man had remarked, "God knows," to which Sam made his reply.

The man was so perturbed by Sam's comment that he finally, in an aggressive manner, posed the question:

"What do you mean, you know?"

Despite the man's intuitive nature, he had no idea as to the can of worms he had just opened.

Sam then explained, "I know because I am Him... I know all that we are and all that we do. I know that deep down inside you are ready to give your life over to me and follow me as your Lord and Savior."

There was silence. Nearly everyone around us was witnessing this conversation unfold. Carol had just walked over to where I was standing to see what all the commotion was about.

"Oh no," Carol whispered into my ear amidst the silence.

"This is bad. Something is not right."

I didn't agree or disagree, but I wondered what she meant.

Then, all of a sudden, out of nowhere, a 6-inch, 7-layer burrito came flying in the air and landed right on Sam, hitting him square in the face. I was watching this in slow motion thanks to some mood elevators that I had also taken, and after the burrito had hit Sam, I reveled in the majestic brilliance of each layer of burrito falling perfectly off Sam's face onto the floor. It was as if the impact of the burrito and Sam's head disrupted the integrity of the burrito itself—in a way that each layer fell one after the other in amazing harmony down to the ground.

There was silence again. This time, everyone in the bar stopped what they were doing.

Finally, without moving a muscle, Sam began to laugh a hearty, joyous laugh. He was not angry, like the flying burrito had knocked some last-minute sense into him. Many of the bar patrons were also laughing. It was a wonderful time. But then, out of the corner of my left eye, I spotted trouble.

Carol nudged me to look, but my eyes had already locked on them. It was the Shadow Orbs. Within seconds, Sam stopped laughing and seemed to be gasping for air.

He clutched at his chest. Then his arms went limp, and he collapsed. Calamity Sam was dead. Heart failure, they said, but I knew the truth. The Shadow Orbs stole his heart for trying to be too much like God. It was justice for the Shadow Orbs and for God, I suppose. It was an injustice for Sam and for me and Carol since Sam was our friend.

After Sam died, a policeman found me and gave me Calamity Sam's journal. The most intriguing entry is confusing to me, so I included it below. Unlike Carol, I could never truly believe anything Calamity Sam ever said, mostly because of his Calamity Proposition. His stories were never based on facts but on information he acquired throughout his life. Either conveniently or out of necessity for emotional or spiritual survival, Sam would always make himself the protagonist. Calamity Sam had a big imagination.

Calamity Sam and the Flying Burrito

Segment from the Journal of Calamity Sam

Today was a weird one, "Journal," hehehe. I think I saw some cool people today, but it's all hazy now, and I don't really remember who they were. These days, we have been livin' in an abandoned apartment. We'll be cool 'til they weed us out, which they always do. For now, though, my flock has a shepherd, and my sheep have shelter. People around town are starting to understand my position and my reasons for calamity. The highlight of the day was the dogs.

You see these dogs come up from the alley—I could see from my window—they converged on this family of raccoons. This happened just before sunrise. Katerina was there when the dogs came. I remember this because she had been calling after her, "friend," Carol. I saw her outside of my window. Kat had spotted a frog and called out to Carol. "Carol, Carol, Carol!!!" she called.

I yelled at Kat to look at the wild dogs ripping this family of raccoons to shreds. She looked, but acted as if she didn't see anything. I wonder... It all looked real to me. Anyway, if I see things, then so does Katerina. Her, "friend," Carol, ain't even real. I ain't got the heart to tell her, but then again, I don't really know... Hey! They gave out free popcorn at the library today. The town library is located in ultra-sunny Simpsons, Colorado. The beautiful old money town located in the south of the state. But you already know all this. Until next time, "Journal." Hehehe. Sam.

The Forests

So one fateful summer, Sam died of heart failure. He was not crucified as Carol and I believed he someday would be. One night, we were at a local bar where we lived—one that was lenient with the homeless and malcontents of the world. We were fine as long as we stayed cool and ordered drinks while we were there. We would often trade our medications for beers and shots when we were broke, and this all made sense to us. We did this on so many nights. But on one fateful night, things took a dark, shadowy turn for me, Carol, and especially Sam. Rest in peace, Calamity Sam, you will certainly be missed, even if you were crazy as hell.

Simpsons, Colorado

Chapter Four: The Quest

The months that followed were especially dark for me. I would have vivid nightmares featuring the ever-looming Shadow Orbs that I could not escape from while I slept. And something else bothered me. I just couldn't believe what I had read in Sam's journal.

Carol...not real? How dare Sam write that? He was one to talk. The story about the dog was completely fabricated. I think about all the times Sam helped us, always gesturing to Carol and me. I just can't fathom the thought that Carol, my best friend, was simply a figment of my imagination. She just had to be real. After all, she was always there when I awoke from my nightmares, to comfort me and tell me it would be alright.

One time, I asked Carol if she was real or someone I perpetually imagined to be real, and this is what she said.

"Oh, that's not really a question, is it? I'm as real as you, Kat, whether I'm in your head or not. Your mind is your reality. Oh, and most importantly, I'm as real as the Shadow Orbs," said Carol, assuredly.

If the Shadow Orbs were real, then so was Carol? That was good enough for me. I needed Carol's help if I was to ever rid myself of the evil Shadow Orbs. Carol was my only connection to what these Shadow Orbs were. She was the only one, besides me, who could see them. As long as I had Carol, I could beat this and find the parts of my life that were lost.

After reading Sam's journal and choosing to believe that Carol was real and not made up, as Sam had suggested, I finally decided to take action. It was time for me to embark on a quest.

The parts of my life that mattered or used to matter—I had to find them. To understand my present and potentially shape my future, I needed to explore my past.

"How would I acquire these things, these parts, these fragments?" I asked Carol.

Instead of a straight answer, Carol looked directly into my eyes and replied, "I have to go... You won't be seeing me for a while, but you will find what was lost. I promise. Remember, your mind is your reality."

She then walked out the door of my small apartment, and when I walked out to see her leave, she was already gone. What I feared in the back of my mind all along was to unexpectedly lose Carol, and it happened. I would have to embark on this quest of mine alone, for the first time since I was lying in a hospital bed for nine months. I thought about my condition and all I knew about my life before the accident. Records indicated that I had previously worked at Avenada's Cosmetics.

The Shadow Orbs at Night

Chapter Five: Shadow Trappers

I traveled by bus back then. It was a good chance to sit and relax, crowded as it was. Thinking about how abruptly Carol seemingly vanished from my life was strange indeed. At one point, during the bus ride, I think I must have been asleep. I had a nightmarish dream. It was a dream that started off as a nightmare but ended in a dream. At first, I felt pain—fears associated with the loss of Sam and now Carol. Then, in my dream, I saw a beautiful sunrise, mixed with leftover darkness from the night before, still pushing its way up and away into the sky. It was then that I woke up, and not a moment too late or too soon. Finally, I had reached my destination.

After about 30 minutes of just standing in front of Avenada's cosmetics, I worked up the courage to walk in. I was greeted by a smiling woman, who I later learned was named Maxine. I'll never forget that smile. The kind of smile that makes one think about the green mountains during spring. Then something random occurred.

Another woman, whom I had never met before, collided with me. She was carrying boxes of cosmetics or something and had too many boxes than she should have.

"Whoa!" She exclaimed. "I'm so sorry, but my boxes slipped. Are you okay?"

I said I was and asked if she needed help with her boxes.

"Oh no, I don't need any help; I have Maxine if I need some help. Maxi! Could you please assist me?" she said, speaking into her radio. "My name is Lisa. I can help you with whatever you need."

Lisa was exquisitely beautiful. Perfect hair, greenish eyes, and that quintessential hourglass figure made Lisa seem so much more majestic than her role as manager of a cosmetics store. She could have been a fairy princess. I engaged her in conversation and accepted her offer of assistance.

"Actually, maybe you can help; my name is Katerina Chen." I worked here once, and now I have returned."

I couldn't believe how awkward I sounded and what I said. Maybe I should have stayed on my medications, but since Carol left me, I just wanted to see everything clearly and hopefully not miss anything. I have to bring this up because it was during this time that I stopped taking my medication for schizophrenia.

"If you need to process a return, Maxine can help you with that," said Lisa.

"Oh no, I don't have anything to return; I have returned. See, I used to work here. I know this must sound really weird, but I am on a quest to find out what my old life was like."

"Do you think maybe you could show me around?" I asked.

"Well, sure. You said you used to work here, and your name is Katerina. When did you last work here?" asked Lisa.

"It was like nine years ago or something. I was in a car accident, and things have not been the same since." I explained.

"Wow! That's crazy. I am sorry to hear about that. It must have been awful," said Lisa.

"Yes, it was very, very awful." I said.

"But you look great; looking at you, I can't even tell you were in a car accident!" said Lisa, as she smiled at me gingerly.

"Thanks," I said. "So what's your story, if I may ask?"

"Well, most people say I have a big heart. I care more about helping other people above anything else, but aside from that, I love cosmetics as well as my independence. Oh, and I love my car! Ooh, sorry, I didn't mean to mention cars," said Lisa.

"Hahaha, it's okay." I said, laughing. I mean, the accident was so long ago, and I was on a quest to find what was lost.

"Hahaha!" Lisa laughed.

"Cars, cars, cars!" She said, jokingly.

"Hahahaha!" I laughed uncontrollably.

Lisa and I continued to make each other laugh, and it seemed as though I had made a friend.

Later on, Lisa would show me around the store to see if I could have a flashback or something to awaken my past memories.

"Ever since my accident, I've been trying to remember my past. If you show me around, maybe I will have a flashback or two. Would that be too much trouble?" I asked.

"Okay," said Lisa. "You can shadow me today; we're kind of slow, so I wouldn't mind at all. In fact, something about you is different. I get a strange magnetic feeling around you. It's so cool!"

"Thanks, Lisa. We're a perfect pair, aren't we? Hahaha," I said jokingly.

Later on, I confessed to Lisa my story of how I lost my friends Carol and Sam. Lisa looked me in the eyes and gave me a big hug.

"I know what it's like to lose people," said Lisa.

It was at that moment that I felt real peace. A blissful, sensational feeling overtook me. No medications, no drugs, no alcohol—just a real connection, and most importantly, no Shadow Orbs.

Perhaps my past and the damage to my memories were to blame, but I could not remember a single moment in my life when I felt that good. Surreal magic was in the air. Lisa and I were both swept up in each other's magnetic field. We became inseparable.

The connection between us was so magnetic that I even forgot that I had schizophrenia. I had lost Carol and Sam, but I had become engulfed in an exceptional friendship with Lisa, and it was changing me for the better.

Over the next several months, I took on a part-time job—my old job at the cosmetics store, in fact—just to be closer to Lisa.

Actually, it was Lisa's idea! After all, Lisa was the one who hired me. I also thought I would have flashbacks as to when I used to work at the cosmetics store, but this was not so. All the joy and contentment of being with Lisa made me forget about the past for good. Or so I thought.

Lisa

This next part is a hard one to explain.

I will not mention anything else private that Lisa and I shared together, for I believe that these things should be kept private and are no one else's business. But I feel there is one story I must tell that is very private. It involves the end of our relationship as well as our last moments together.

In the last six months of our relationship, Lisa had garnered the courtship of a male customer who was a business owner. He had charm, style, and lots of money. He made advances with Lisa in the romantic sense whenever he came to the store. She liked him, and began dating him. Lisa was quite smitten with her wealthy prince. Lisa began thinking that he was going to propose to her.

Before the last big date, Lisa asked for my opinion on the matter.

"It's a great idea," I said to Lisa. "You could marry him and be rich, and I'd be 'happening,' for you. I just hope I will still be able to see you."

I meant to say 'happy,' but it came out 'happening.'

"Oh, don't worry, Kat, I'd be 'happening' for you too, hahaha," she said, smiling. "You'd be my bride's maid, and we'll still be best friends; I'll just have a rich, charming husband on the side, hahaha," she laughed.

I could tell Lisa was extremely happy and excited. And she was definitely serious. I laughed too. Despite my personal feelings, I was happy for Lisa.

On a Saturday night, Lisa went out with her wealthy, stylish suitor. Although this time, something did not go right.

"No, no, no! How could I be so stupid? Why like this? Why like this?!" Lisa screamed.

"Lisa, you're hurt. My God, what happened?" I asked as I embraced her.

We just sat there, holding each other for a few minutes. I then looked down and noticed Lisa's black eye.

"Oh no, Lisa." I paused. "I can make this right. You tell me where he is, and I will find him and get him back. Nobody hurts my Lisa!" I proclaimed.

Lisa looked at me and smiled, but didn't nod any approval. Lisa then looked away from me and started telling me what happened, as if she were reliving it in her mind.

"Everything was so perfect. He actually popped the question. But I… I hesitated, and then I told him no. He became angry, as if I had just committed an evil act against him. And then he became violent. He kept asking me why not, and when I told him I wasn't sure, he erupted. After what seemed like hours, he carried me outside, tossed me into a limousine, and I was taken home." Lisa then looked up at me with sadness in her eyes and said,

"He never even said goodbye."

Lisa cried.

"It is not the abuse that hurts. Kat…it was… There was no empathy from him, not even a hint of it, and I don't know why I said no," explained Lisa grimacingly.

"Lisa, why did you say no? Can you tell me, please?" I asked.

"I was… I was thinking… I couldn't stop thinking about you, Kat. I couldn't stop thinking that if I married him, then I would never see you again. I love you," said Lisa. We embraced one another. I loved her too.

Finally, Lisa looked at me and told me she was in a lot of pain. Lisa then asked if there was something I could do for her.

"Anything, Lisa, you name it." I said.

"Well, I know you told me you had schizophrenia and used to take medication for it. Would it be possible if we could take some of those painkillers that you mentioned?"

Asked Lisa. "It's just that I am in a lot of pain, both physically and emotionally."

"Well, sure, I have some here with me. For a while, I didn't take them at all, so I have lots now." I said.

I had no idea Lisa was going to ask for this, but it made sense. If there was ever a time to take painkillers, well, now was a good time. Except that these were not ordinary painkillers; they were actually antipsychotics. They achieved the same desired result, but with wild, more extreme potential side effects.

So Lisa and I partied all night and had a really good time for a while. We started drinking alcohol at some point—straight vodka. Everything was getting a little better and a little better.

Later, we added ecstasy to the mix and threw our phones out of the sixth-floor window of our apartment. We danced, sang, and enjoyed each other's company. We went late into the night until it was almost sunrise, and finally, pop!

All of a sudden, Lisa dropped to the ground, clutching her chest, the same way I had seen happen to Sam. I would have tried to call an ambulance, but as I mentioned, we had thrown our phones out the window in a fit of passion earlier in the night. Our phones were history.

At the same time, I hear a knock on the door. Ignoring the door and crouching down to try and help Lisa, I notice out of the corner of my eye, someone enters our apartment.

The door was locked, I thought, but maybe it wasn't. I turned Lisa over, as she was beginning to vomit while simultaneously going through some sort of cardiac arrest. She was still breathing at this point when the figure who had entered our apartment touched me on the shoulder.

"Hello stranger."

... It was Carol!

"Carol!" I cried, "You have to help me. We mixed antipsychotic drugs with vodka and ecstasy, and now I think my friend Lisa is dying. Please, what should I do?"

"Look," Carol said as she pointed at the ceiling.

I looked up at the ceiling, and I could see them. It was the Shadow Orbs.

"Your friend Lisa was a good, honest human being; the Shadow Orbs will take her when they have no right to. If they succeed, then they will be trapped forever. But...you have to let her go," explained Carol.

"If you're telling me that I have a choice, then I choose to save my best friend!" I screamed.

All at once, I leapt into the air and out of the apartment. I started yelling for help and banging on doors. An old man came out of his apartment to see what was going on. I told him what was happening, and he immediately called for the ambulance. But it was too late.

As the ambulance pulled up, Lisa turned to me and, in her four final breaths, said,

"I. Love. You. Kat."

It was as if she was trying so hard just to speak each word. I watched her die in my arms.

"It is a sad thing, Katerina Chen, but the Shadow Orbs have been trapped forever, and you will never see them again. All hail Lisa, the Shadow Trapper. May she rest in peace," said Carol.

As Carol said this, I felt a swelling of pride in my heart. Pride for Lisa to sacrifice herself in order to trap the Shadow Orbs, overdosing herself for me. I climbed up the escape ladder to the rooftop of the apartment complex and shouted,

"All hail Lisa, the Shadow Trapper!!!"

All Hail Lisa, The Shadow Trapper!

Chapter Six: Hypnosis

After Lisa died, I decided it was time to leave, and I left quickly. The authorities would eventually do an autopsy and discover the leftover drugs in Lisa's system. This could potentially lead them to me, so I left. The sadness and grief were enough, but I was past that. Lisa had made the ultimate sacrifice and became the Shadow Trapper. Now all I had to do was start over. This time I headed to the American West Coast. Something was calling me to California; I just didn't know what it was.

I arrived via bus transportation, right smack in the middle of San Diego. There was a university that I wanted to visit. On the bus ride, I met someone who informed me of research going on at a major university in San Diego—a schizophrenia research study. I thought, well, if these new drugs or therapies work, then maybe it will help me remember, and rid me of the Shadow Orbs once and for all. Since Lisa's death, the Shadow Orbs had returned. I knew something wasn't right so maybe seeking real treatment was the right course of action. It wasn't something I planned, but this talk of schizophrenia research certainly applied to me. It did not matter. What mattered was that it was something.

I wandered into a courtyard filled with glorious landscaping and suddenly realized I was at the university. I looked in different directions at the various buildings. I walked up to one of the closer buildings and gazed at a statue of Sigmund Freud, the late psychologist. I surmised that this was the building where psychology and other social sciences must be taught. I took a deep breath and walked inside.

At the end of the hall, there was a room where people were coming and going. I walked down to the room and discovered this was where to sign up for the schizophrenia study. As I walked in, I could feel eyes on me, but not the general social paranoia. This was different. I could feel a specific set of eyes on me.

As I waited in a line of people, it dawned on me that all of these people must have had schizophrenia like I did. I never knew there were so many. I shut my eyes and tried to listen for who was watching me. I turned around sharply while opening my eyes to see if I could catch the person eyeing me down. When I looked, I saw a man who looked about the same age as me, if I were to guess. I approached him.

"For what reason were you eyeing me?" I asked.

"You look familiar," he said. "Are you here for the study?"

"Why yes, I am familiar, huh? Well, I don't recall you, but then again, I've had a lot of changes take place with my memory over the years." I said.

"That's perfect! Our study focuses on a participant's memory deduction and memory recognition while experiencing symptoms of schizophrenia. Do you have schizophrenia? And may I ask your name?" he said.

"I'm Katerina Chen, and I have schizophrenia... It comes and goes, the result of a car accident almost ten years ago." I explained and then asked, "What's a participant?"

"If you agree to participate in our study, we will compensate you. It is five days per week, sometimes less, and lasts for twelve weeks. Step one is to determine if each participant is actually schizophrenic. Our teams of doctors and psychoanalysts will evaluate each participant and provide an appropriate diagnosis. Would you be interested? By the way, my name is Robbie," he explained, as I noticed other possible participants were in conversations with other scholarly types like himself all around me at this point.

"Hmm," I said, "I'll have to think about it."

Then I smiled at him and said,

"Okay, I'll do it; where do I sign?"

After all, it was why I was there.

Robbie smiled and handed me a clipboard with many forms attached for me to fill out. Robbie and I continued speaking while I filled out form after form, which he helped me with all the way through. The more he spoke, the more I felt like he was familiar too, but I just couldn't place it. Perhaps this study would provide the treatment I needed to unlock my memories from the past. Perhaps my memories are in good condition and merely require adjustment and organization. One thing is for sure, though: living with schizophrenia and treating it are two bipolar things.

Robbie

We were now on the first day of the study, which was a basic diagnosis.

"May I ask your name for the record?" asked Robbie.

"Katerina Chen," I replied.

"How old are you, and where were you born? Asked Robbie.

"I'm 32, and I was born in Santa Barbara, California," I said.

"How long have you had schizophrenia?" Asked Robbie.

"For about ten years now, ever since my car accident," I replied.

"Tell me about the accident," said Robbie.

"It was awful. I was in a coma for three weeks, reliving it in my mind. I was in a hospital bed for nine months afterwards. I lost my mind, forgot who I was, and still struggle with my memories," I explained.

I could tell this wasn't going to be an easy part of the study. Little did I know, the hardest parts were yet to come because I hadn't mentioned Carol, Sam, Lisa, or the Shadow Orbs.

"And how many 'traumatic' events have you experienced in your life since the accident, living with schizophrenia?" Asked Robbie.

"Wow, that's a tough one," I said. "If I were to put a number on it, not counting the accident, maybe 127."

"127?" Robbie asked, amazed.

I could tell Robbie was astounded by the figure I gave him. I guess I had to come clean. I opened up to Robbie about the Shadow Orbs, Carol, Sam, Lisa, and all the insane nightmares and instances where the lines of fantasy and reality blurred in real-life situations. And they usually did not end well.

The number I estimated had to be in the hundred or so range because I'd been encountering the shadows almost every week for nearly a decade at that point. Robbie finished his prognosis and then asked if we could conduct the last part of day one of the study. He asked me to sign one more form for a specific reason. I was going to be hypnotized.

"I want you to close your eyes and listen to my voice," said Robbie, speaking with a more solemn, dreamy tone.

I was lying down on the therapy house couch, as I named it, feeling very relaxed. I was drifting into a dream state, as Robbie's words seemed to relieve all resistance or tension that would have prevented me from doing so.

"I want you to try to remember before your accident, before your schizophrenia, and look slowly. We are traversing the inner depths of your mind to the center of your memory core. Look. See. Feel. Remember," said Robbie as he continued his enchantment.

"All I see is colors," I exclaimed.

I could see myself in my mind's eye. I was looking, seeing, and feeling, but all I could see was colors, and I could still not see anything related to my memories.

"Ahhh!!! AAhhh!!! AAAhhhhh!!!!!" I cried.

The colors were stabbing me, shouting at me in gibberish. I just couldn't take it. Suddenly, I woke up. I looked around, and I was standing over Robbie. To my left was a broken lamp. Did I do this?

All at once, I remembered the nightmare I was just having. I used the lamp to ward off the colors. The lamp must have accidentally connected with poor Robbie in the real world. That's why the lamp was broken, and that's why Robbie was knocked out. It was amazing and curious at the same time—how I could somehow logically piece together a conclusion so quickly after doing something crazy. But perhaps I was wrong.

"Robbie," I said, lightly tapping the side of his face to try and wake him up.

"Robbie, wake up." Wake up, Robbie."

Robbie swiftly awoke from his knocked-out state.

"Whoa, Katerina? Am I awake?" asked Robbie, apparently dazed and confused.

"Yes, it's alright. I'm here. Are you okay?" I asked, with a look of guilt entrapping my face.

"Yes, I feel fine. The last thing I remember is that you stood up and began speaking. And did you hit me with a lamp? Asked Robbie, now holding his head.

I was shocked, but ultimately knew the truth.

"Y-yes, I believe I did. I am truly sorry. If it makes you feel better, I wasn't aiming for you." I explained to Robbie.

"Well, that's good, and it's okay. I'm used to this. Well not really used to it, but you're not the first real schizophrenic patient I've encountered, or rather, tried to hypnotize or treat," said Robbie.

I could feel Robbie was sincere as well as understanding what I had just been through without really seeing it for himself.

"Robbie," I started, "Did you notice anything while you were unconscious?" I asked, as I was almost certain there was more to this than just another schizophrenic episode.

"Now that you mention it... colors. I saw different flashing colors," said Robbie.

I gasped. Were these the same colors from my dream, I wondered?

"Robbie, did you see me or yourself looking at these colors in your mind?" I asked.

"No," said Robbie, "just flashing colors."

"Robbie," this time I spoke like a detective interrogating a witness,

"Do you think it is possible that we could be linked somehow through our dreams—like some kind of psychic connection?"

"Well," began Robbie,

"That is definitely a theory... I think it is safe to say that you have schizophrenia, and after years of working with patients with schizophrenia, maybe I'm a little bit schizophrenic too. I would like to invite you to participate in the rest of the study. I think if there is a psychic link connecting us through our dreams, then this program could benefit both of us. Perhaps I can assist you in remembering and resolving your nightmares. Maybe together we can help you find what was lost."

The Stabbing Colors

Chapter Seven: Memory Juice

The schizophrenia study was a grueling up-and-down cycle of different medications, hours of talks with the doctors, and back and forth with Robbie, whom I had grown to care for as I learned more about him. He was a younger doctor, a real psychologist, and an experienced hypnotist, and yet something about him was so familiar that it drove me crazy.

One time, I asked Robbie about his childhood, and he explained that he had many siblings growing up since his father had five different wives, all by the time he was twenty. That's a new partner every four years. This was interesting enough, but when Robbie probed me about my childhood, I admitted that I too had many different siblings growing up, but there was not one memory from my childhood that I could confidently draw upon. There was simply nothing there. In about the tenth week of the study, Robbie came to me with a surprise.

"Check this out," said Robbie, noticeably excited.

"We have this new medication that is a fluid; you drink it, and I can't wait to see the test results. Furthermore, and perhaps most importantly, this medication has the potential to significantly improve your health. If it works, the applications could fundamentally cure schizophrenia, as well as a vast variety of other mind-related conditions. Are you ready?"

Hmm. I imagined it for a moment before agreeing. I saw myself in the center of my mind's eye—remembering, knowing, and confident in my ability to recall things again. No more paranoia; no more restless nights from delusions and traumatic events I've experienced over the last ten years. Yes, I thought I was ready. For Lisa, Carol, and Sam.

Somehow I was drawn here, and now quite possibly I could be cured. I could finally find what was lost.

"So I just drink it?" I inquired, now concerned about the potential risks associated with this treatment.

"Yes, and drink it all in one sitting, otherwise it may not work," Robbie said.

"Are there any possible side effects?" I asked, feeling more curious than usual.

"Of course, there is always a possibility of side effects from any drug, but with this drink, whatever happens, it's liquid, and your body will eventually pass it through the urinary tract. Any side effects you may experience will be temporary. We will position you on our couch, monitoring your brain impulses with a special helmet that contains nodes connected to your head. It will knock you out rather quickly.

As you fall asleep, you will hear my voice through the mini-speaker in the helmet you'll be wearing. I will suggest specific keywords just to jog your memories—not hypnosis. I'll be in the next room the whole time, so there will be minimal distractions while you're under. This could be it." Robbie explained.

"Alright," I said, "but how will I know if it's working?" I asked.

"Simple—you won't, or maybe you will in your mind. At any rate, we'll look at the results together afterwards, and I'll ask you some questions after each session." said Robbie.

The helmet was the Mod-7. It was technologically more advanced than a regular CAT scan of the brain. I liked the Mod-7 helmet. It was comfortable, warm, and inviting. The Mod-7 was also inviting to brain stimuli and various natural impulses and seemed to help me with general stress release whenever I would use it. Each time I used the Mod-7, my confidence in the treatments and therapy sessions grew. I was here for a reason, and my optimism was firing on all cylinders.

"Hey," I asked. "So what do you call this stuff?"

"Well, the other doctors each have their own names for it—different technical names. I like to refer to it simply as memory juice. It is a concentrate of the top twenty natural mind-affecting substances and medicines combined into one treatment," explained Robbie.

"Okay," I said, "I'm ready. Let's do this!"

Robbie handed me the first vial of Memory Juice. I would take this stuff for the next five days. I laid down on the couch provided for me, put on my Mod-7, and drank the first vial.

"Bottoms up," I said to Robbie as I drank the first vial confidently.

As I started to fall deeper and deeper asleep, I remember hearing Robbie's soft voice telling me to remember and then listing several keywords from my past, almost spoken at a whisper. His voice was in my head now, and I could feel the memory juice reorganizing my brain.

Finally, there was nothing. I could no longer hear Robbie's voice in my head as colors of all different hues began to flood my mind. My mind was filled with hues of purple, followed by red, then pink, orange, yellow, green, and blue. Then the colors stopped. They had mixed into one giant tie-dye explosion in my mind. Then the colors went away. I was back in my movie.

There I was as a 9-year-old again, playing in a sandbox. And I wasn't alone. There was also a boy who appeared to be the same age playing in the sandbox with me. Who was he? If I kept watching my movie, then maybe I'd find out. Then two grown-up figures appeared as if out of nowhere. It was my mother and a father figure who was not my father.

"Katerina! Katerina!" I heard a voice calling me, and it was my mother. "Kat, Robbie, come inside. It's going to rain."

Rain? I looked around, and it was a sunny afternoon. Where were the signs of this rain? I looked at Robbie. Was this the same Robbie, or maybe he was there because of the treatment, and I was imagining him?

"KORACARUNCHH!" A vicious, roaring thunder cut sharply throughout my mind. Rain was coming, or something was coming...

"KORACARUNCHH!" sounded the thunder again.

Oh no, this can't be real. I remember thinking this must have been a side effect of the memory juice. I also remember feeling helpless and scared at that moment. I was lying there, feeling tormented by my schizophrenic condition and unable to do anything about this nightmarish thunder.

"KORACARUNCHH!"

No, it knows. It knows about me. It knows about Carol, Lisa and Sam. It knows about the Shadow Orbs. Make it stop! Make it stop! I was now trembling with fear. In that moment, I remember hearing the thunder grow louder and louder, getting closer to my childhood flashback setting. And there was no rain. Instead, a bright, blinding light appeared, breaking up into an oval-shaped doorway of sorts. I climbed in through this oval-shaped doorway. I had just managed to escape the thunder.

Inside, it was a separate world. On the other side, I could still see the sandbox and Robbie through the oval-shaped doorway. He waved at me, signaling that this was goodbye. I waved back, somehow knowing the dream was about to change again. Inside the oval-shaped doorway was nothing but a large, multi-colored robe. I wrapped the large, multi-colored robe around myself as I sat, waiting in that endless void of nothingness. It was at this point that I woke up.

"How are you feeling, Katerina? Are you alright?" Asked Robbie. He was in the room with me in his chair as I took off my Mod-7 helmet.

"I'm fine, I guess. How long was I out?"

"Nine hours," he said. "I have a medical team standing by. We thought you were in a coma."

What!? Nine hours!? Could I truly have experienced real-time fear and trepidation while listening to the thunder and sitting in the void with my blanket for nine hours? This was insane. The memory juice was some powerful stuff.

I looked at Robbie, gave him a good hard look, and asked,

"Robbie, did you used to be my brother?"

Robbie was not expecting this type of question.

Suddenly, he realized that perhaps the memory juice had worked on the first try.

"I don't know. Maybe we should do some sort of investigation—pull up background checks, that sort of thing. Both of our parents have remarried more than several times. We both confessed to having many different siblings growing up. Was I in your dream state?"

It was like he knew, but he didn't want to say.

"Yes," I exclaimed, "you were there, and so was I. Do you recall playing with me in the sandbox when we were nine years old?"

The look on his face was priceless. His mouth was open, and his eyes widened.

"Oh my God, Katerina, I do remember! It's as if a light just went off in my brain. We were brother and sister once," Robbie exclaimed, "when we were both nine!"

"Robbie, I remember you now. I was drawn to this school and this place. At the time, I did not remember you, but I was seemingly brought here for a reason. By the way, that's some good memory juice." I said, smiling.

"You could say that again," said Robbie. "You're taking the magical memory juice, and yet somehow I'm remembering things—magnificent! We will still run some tests. You were not supposed to be out that long, so we should proceed with caution. But I am glad it's working," said Robbie as he grabbed a mop from a nearby closet.

Apparently, I had been out so long that I was urinating the memory juice out during this nine-hour period.

"Oh my goodness, I am so sorry!" I exclaimed.

But Robbie told me not to worry. In fact, he said if I hadn't released the memory juice naturally, then I would most certainly be in a coma by now. Robbie explained that it took approximately nine hours for the memory juice to leave my system, which is the only reason I was able to wake up.

The Oval Doorway

Chapter Eight: Dream State

The last day of Memory Juice was on a Friday. After nearly three weeks and fifteen vials, I had remembered so much about my childhood and my previous relationships. Even more importantly, I discovered why I had really gone to the West Coast—to reunite with my lost stepbrother, Robbie, psychologist extraordinaire. Robbie was helping me with my schizophrenia, and up to this point, I had made real progress. Perhaps I could be cured.

"Okay, Kat, this is the last day of the memory juice, for now anyway. In six months, based on the results, we could potentially achieve significant academic recognition. Katerina Chen and Robbie Manning will become household names. As our key participant in this study, you will share in the glory of being the first person ever completely cured of schizophrenia," said Robbie.

"Oh, you know, I don't care about any glory, just the results," I said.

"I know," said Robbie, "but it's fair for you to get some of the credit; I just hope it works as a viable long-term treatment or maybe..." Robbie paused, as I could tell he was deep in thought about something.

"What? What is it?" I asked.

"This will be the very last time you ever need treatment!" Robbie exclaimed.

What a thought. To think I could be cured of my nightmares, my past delusions, and the trauma brought on by those evil Shadow Orbs. I felt relieved, anxious, and optimistic all at the same time. What a cool revelation.

"Robbie," I began, "what if it doesn't work? What if I have to drink this stuff for the rest of my life?" I asked.

"Well, then I would have to make memory juice for the rest of my life, wouldn't I?" He replied. "If it becomes a standard treatment for schizophrenia someday, then I'll gladly be making memory juice for the rest of my life."

I smiled. Robbie had my best interests at heart, as well as the best interests of his future patients, who could potentially benefit from the memory juice.

"Okay, Robbie, it's go-time. Where's my drink?" I said.

I put on my Mod-7 brain scan helmet and drank the last vial for the study. Robbie had everything set up, and we were ready. He started with my selected keywords, which had now been narrowed down to just three words. "Discover...Rekindle...Truth," Robbie whispered through my helmet's mini speaker.

I drifted quickly; the colors came and tie-dyed again, much faster than ever, and within what seemed like mere moments, I had reached my destination.

Inside the deepest contours of my brain's memory center, I saw a statue emblazoned with what appeared to me to be a real gold coating. The statue's head was that of a wolf. It was the golden wolf. What did it mean? I gazed at this wonderful statue head for a while. I had seen it before at a zoo. I was on a date. With whom I could not remember, but this statue I had seen.

While peering into the eyes of the Golden Wolf, a cabin must have formed. I looked to my left, and there it was. The front door of the cabin opened, and a bright, blinding light appeared, much like the first one I had seen during my experience with my first vial of Memory Juice. This time, however, someone came through the door and passed through the light into view. It was a beautiful woman from my memory.

"Lisa." I spoke aloud.

"Katerina, I have to tell you something," said Lisa, glowing in a way I had never seen her glow before. I knew she was a fairy princess! Lisa was now standing right in front of me.

"My soul is at peace now, and I've been sent to help you remember... Lisa continued, "I've been sent to help you remember and to give you strength in the days to come."

"The Golden Wolf symbolizes the happiest time in your life before the accident. You were on a date with a man you loved. But there is a reason why you have blocked the memory of the golden wolf until now. It is because this man, whom you loved and who also loved you, died several months later of suicide. As you will now recall, his wife refused to grant him a divorce and made several threats to your life. Your would-be love was found dead of carbon monoxide poisoning in his car, with a note taped to his chest. You should remember this: His suicide note was also his confession of his undying love for you, but as he remarked in the note, he was not strong enough to run away with you." explained Lisa.

"Why are you telling me this, Lisa?" I managed to ask with tears in my eyes, somehow remembering all of this.

"Every time you remember a negative or traumatic experience from your past, the memory juice allows you to resolve it here in your dream state. This memory is one of your worst ones, so I had to remind you of it," said Lisa.

I started crying again, but this time it came from an immense guilt that I was suddenly feeling for Lisa's death.

"Lisa… I'm so sorry I gave you those pills. I'm so sorry you died… I'm just so… sorry," I said to Lisa as she looked into my eyes lovingly the whole time.

"Kat, it's okay," Lisa replied. "I asked for it; I literally asked you for those pills. You're not the reason I'm dead. I am. From what I recall, you tried to save me. And I remember telling you, I loved you with my last bit of life, and… I will always love you, Katerina Chen."

I felt the guilt wash away. This memory juice really helped me get through all of those feelings and bad memories. It was at this moment that I understood what had happened to me. My schizophrenia, which allowed me to see the Shadow Orbs, nightmares, and delusions for the last ten years, was just a transformation of all my traumatic experiences prior to my accident. The Memory Juice had helped me reveal the truth, reconcile my past, and discover who I was and ultimately still am.

"But there is more, Kat." Lisa spoke again, this time with a more solemn tone, and it also appeared that her brightness had faded just enough to be noticeable.

"I told you my soul was free. I helped you remember. Now I'm going to give you strength," said Lisa.

"Strength?" I asked, knowing there was bad news to come.

"Yes, strength. My spirit will be with you when you need me most, " said Lisa.

"What's going to happen?" I asked.

Lisa hugged me, and it felt so real. She finally looked into my eyes and spoke.

"Listen, Kat, My soul is free now. I was the Shadow Trapper. But now that my soul is free, the last of the Shadow Orbs has been released, and it is the worst one. You will wake up soon, and when you do, be careful. The last Shadow Orb will be coming for you, but this time for good. It was here, in your dream state, but it's on the outside now. It has immense power, and this last Shadow Orb's attachment to you will only increase, blurring your reality until you finally witness the ultimate...evil."

"The ultimate evil?" I said, in wonder and confusion.

As soon as I spoke, Lisa disappeared. Then there was a loud noise like an alarm going off in my dream state, and I could also smell smoke. What was going on? I wondered. I looked around, trying to detect the noise and odor, when a whirlwind of tie-dyed colors in the shape of a

small tornado came and swept me away.

The Golden Wolf

Chapter Nine: Third World Debt

Inside the psychology building, I awoke to discover the noise and odor from my dream state. There was a fire and smoke. It was real. Then I thought about what Lisa had said about my last Shadow Orb. I had to be careful. Did my last shadow cause this fire? I had to find out. I looked at my watch to check the time. I had only been out for two hours from the memory juice, and I detected no wetness around the couch where I was lying down. I looked around for Robbie, but I could not find him.

I poked my head out to look into the hallway, and there was indeed a fire. The fire was at the far end of the hallway, conjoining the second corridor and spreading into the nearby classroom and study rooms. I looked around for the nearest exit. If I could get to the back of the building, I could make it. I followed the path furthest from where the fire was, and then I stopped, like a deer in headlights. Exiting the classroom right in front of me was my last Shadow Orb.

I froze, unable to breathe. However, a voice in my head spoke to me. It was Lisa's voice. She was still with me. She told me to use the scalpel. I looked at the ground, and sure enough, there was a scalpel just lying there. Sometimes medical students who also studied surgery would be in here taking certain psychology classes. One of them must have dropped it. I picked up the scalpel.

My last Shadow Orb was looming towards me, but it made no attempt at an attack. It seemed that I was going to have to make the first move.

"Did you start the fire?" I asked, my confidence growing.

There was silence.

"Okay," I said, "I've had it with you, Shadow Orbs."

As I was saying this, I lunged forward, squaring up with my last Shadow Orb. I stabbed and stabbed with all my might until I must have caught something because the scalpel was forced out of my hand. My last Shadow Orb let out a howling sound of pain.

The howling would not stop. So, I ran down the hall and followed the left corridor to the back exit. I had escaped.

Robbie drove a blue Mustang—not typical for a psychologist, I guess—but he once told me he was a car enthusiast and loved cars that had been around for a long time. It was his hobby. He also made an extra key for me in case of emergencies. I looked around the parking lot for Robbie. When I didn't see anyone, I hopped into Robbie's blue Mustang and drove around to see what was going on. I could see fire trucks on their way at full speed, so I drove out of the parking lot away from the building. Then I heard a voice in my head repeatedly telling me to keep driving.

So, I kept driving. The experience I just had with my last Shadow Orb still had me shaking, so I drove. As I pulled up to the exit of the campus, I wondered where exactly I was going.

"Turn left," I heard a voice say.

I looked behind me to the back seat, and there was Carol.

"Carol!?" I exclaimed. I just couldn't believe my eyes. Carol was in the blue Mustang with me the whole time. Where did she come from?

"There is something you must witness. It is an ultimate evil that you must witness for yourself or you will suffer unjustly. We're going to a pier in a secluded area of the West Coast. In the bay area, there will be a fleet of ships from various countries around the world. If you cannot endure this experience, then your spirit will break, and your last Shadow Orb will take you forever. Only once you have seen the greatest crime against humanity will you finally understand the depth of your own struggles. Once this happens, the resolution will naturally take its course. You'll finally be free," explained Carol.

"And there is more," said another voice.

Sitting right next to Carol, in the other back seat, was Lisa.

"Lisa!" I cried, "You're here too?"

"Of course, Kat. I told you I would be here to give you strength going forward. Together, the three of us will witness something horrid in the bay area. The ultimate evil, as Carol mentioned, will most likely cause you to vomit or upset you in a way that affects you both physically and mentally. You must be ready. When you get to the next stoplight, I want you to turn left," explained Lisa.

After we came to a complete stop, Lisa, Carol, and myself gathered our strength in silence as I made the left-hand turn. The road we were on took us west to the coast. As I drove, I began to notice how the road was far from straight. The road bent and twisted so much that I thought I was going to be sick. Lisa wasn't kidding about the vomiting, and we hadn't even arrived at our destination yet.

I imagined that we were not driving on a road, but rather driving on the back of a giant snake, or at least the trail left behind by a giant snake with so many twists and turns.

As we continued driving, I spotted a road sign that read 'Serpent Avenue.' So it was the trail of a giant snake—how bizarre.

We had been driving for 20 minutes or so with total silence amongst the three of us when Carol finally spoke.

"Kat, your rearview mirror, take a look," Carol said.

I looked, and I could not see the road behind us. A dark cloud was behind us, following us as if it were trying to absorb us.

"What is it?" I asked, a bit frightened and unsure if I really wanted to know.

"That," said Lisa, "is your last Shadow Orb. The biggest and the meanest. It knows where we are going and what our plan is. It's alright though; once we see what we are supposed to see, your last Shadow Orb will be destroyed, deflated, and resolved. But you should speed up. It's not far now."

I put the pedal to the metal and sped up. Robbie's blue mustang could really haul. We were at over 100 miles per hour, faster than I had ever driven in my life, when suddenly we hit some kind of speed bump or something protruding out of the road.

"Vroooommm, CRASH!"

We went flying in Robbie's blue Mustang, soaring through the air like a spaceship. Thankfully, when we crashed, all we hit was sand. The blue mustang was stuck about six feet in, but we were okay. We were able to pull ourselves out of the Mustang through the windows since the doors were partially blocked by sand. I looked up and saw my last Shadow Orb move over us and past us out over the bay.

"This is it," said Carol, "we have arrived."

Carol, Lisa, and I walked to the edge of the beach and looked out at the bay past the pier. It was only a few moments before I spotted a fleet of ships coming our way.

As I walked to the edge of the beach to get a closer look at these ships, my foot caught something in the sand. I crouched down to see what it was. I had to dig some of the sand out in order to uncover what appeared to be a spyglass. What were the chances? Someone had left a spyglass in the sand specifically for me to see what I needed to see.

I took a peek through the spyglass and could now see the ships up close. Nations from all over the world hoisted different flags on each ship. I recognized some of the flags—France, Italy, and China—and on board were what looked like people in rags, dirty and sad. Then I spotted a massive ship, which turned out to be a gigantic incinerator!

On the side of this massive incinerator vessel read the words:

"THIRD WORLD DEBT."

The people dressed in rags on the nearby ships were now transported on to the incinerator vessel. Against their will, people dressed in rags were being thrown into the incinerator vessel in groups of two or four. The incinerator's fires and smoke were overwhelming, as more and more people were being burned alive. A power station was located on one end of the incinerator vessel. At the top of this station read the words:

"HUMAN BIOFUELS."

Suddenly, I felt sick. I thought for a moment about what I just saw and lost it. I began to vomit uncontrollably.

Some of what came out I recognized as memory juice. When I was finished, Carol began to speak.

"The big nations of the world come here to burn the poor and helpless of third-world countries as payment for aid. Human biofuels, a unique and efficient form of energy, represent the true value of a human being in this case. This is the ultimate evil. To know that a system we humans have created could become so warped and corrupt that it allows for events like this to take place is unfathomable. You see, Kat, the Shadow Orbs are everywhere. They influence all of the perceived evil that takes place on this planet. You had to witness this because now that you have seen what they are truly capable of, the Shadow Orbs will leave you alone. You have finally seen enough."

The Incinerator Ships

Chapter 10: The Shadow Master

I awoke in a hospital bed. The actual feeling of being born again entered my mind and heart as this wave of internal peace seemed to take me. Robbie was right there, waiting for me to wake up. He mentioned how they found me on the beach with his blue Mustang, half-entrenched in sand. He said that when they found me, I was fast asleep, and all my vital signs were normal.

"How do you feel?" asked Robbie.

"Amazing," I said with a smile.

"How about you?" I asked.

"Doing fine. That fire was completely random and crazy. Apparently, you apprehended the person responsible. He turned himself in right away after you stabbed him."

"My last Shadow Orb..." I said, almost under my breath.

"What?" asked Robbie.

"The person I stabbed... I thought it was my last Shadow Orb," I said.

"Well, that explains everything. Your last Shadow Orb manifested itself in the form of someone who wanted to cause harm to others. You are blessed, Kat, to have such good luck when things seem their worst," said Robbie.

"I had help from Lisa and Carol, whom I doubt I'll ever see again."

"Katerina, are you sure you're alright?" asked Robbie.

"Robbie, I finally feel free. I want to thank you for all your help, bro," I said.

"Hahaha, you're welcome, sis," said Robbie.

We hugged one another, knowing that the nightmare was finally over.

On May 24th, Robbie and I attended a huge ceremony in recognition of World Schizophrenia Day. Both Robbie and I received awards for our contributions to the treatment of schizophrenia. My overall diagnosis was that my schizophrenia had gone into remission. Although I wasn't cured, my condition has significantly improved. Needless to say, I had grown as a person. I had faced traumatic experiences head-on and survived. That was all.

At the ceremony, Robbie gave a breath-taking speech. Attendees included people with schizophrenia like me, doctors, psychologists, scholars, and many others connected to the condition. All of them wanted to meet me.

During the ceremony, Robbie and I found ourselves separated as we interacted with various interesting individuals. One person with whom I spoke was Dr. Swagler. I will never forget our discussion or what followed.

This Dr. Swagler stood out from many others due to his distinctly unflattering demeanor. His breath was awful, and his lack of physical space boundaries was evident. Still, I gave him respect and courtesy and listened to what he had to say.

"Katerina, my treatment of schizophrenia is simply the best. People who are deaf have benefited from it the most. It has to do with sound," said Dr. Swagler.

"Sound? How do you use sound to help with schizophrenia?" I asked.

"Well, it's fascinating that you should inquire; your story about the evasive Shadow Orbs is why I'm here. Would you like to hear what they sound like?" asked Dr. Swagler.

I was speechless. The sound of the Shadow Orbs? I couldn't speak because of anxiety and possible inner dread, so I simply nodded a yes.

Dr. Swagler then pulled out an audio recording device from his front shirt pocket. He pressed play. I listened. It was a very low-toned humming sound, but it was not booming. The sound itself was almost unnatural, somehow producing sound from sources other than the built-in speakers on Dr. Swagler's audio recording equipment. The ceremony was in a large hall; could it be the echo? But it didn't sound like an echo.

"It's not an echo," said Dr. Swagler mischievously, as if he knew what I was thinking.

"It's the altered texture of the soundwaves. It allows the sound you are hearing to transcend the limitations of speaker outputs as well as our own human capacity to hear things," he explained.

I had noticed Dr. Swagler's nasty demeanor and crass appearance, but now he was different. He looked at me straight in the eyes with an evil grin, as if he knew all of my secrets. It was as if the Devil himself had taken hold of this man, for his eyes had changed the most.

Then Dr. Swagler spoke with a deeper, more gravelly tone of voice than before, one that did not sound like his normal voice. His new voice sounded demonic.

"You can never evade the Shadow Orbs, for they are now under my domain. I have unlocked the key to speaking with the Shadow Orbs through the manipulation of soundwaves. Through soundwaves, I can control the appetite of the Shadow Orbs. When they become aggressive, I can ward them off. I can control them. You will work with me to achieve greater understanding of them. You will join me, Katerina Chen, for I am the Shadow Master," proclaimed Dr. Swagler.

Once again, I could not move after hearing this. Was this all just a dream? Who was this, Dr. Swagler? He says he's the Shadow Master?

I looked around for Robbie and spotted him coming towards us. It was almost as if he sensed I was in danger.

When Robbie finally came up to me, I looked for Dr. Swagler, and he was gone. It was as if he had disappeared.

"Are you alright, Kat?" asked Robbie. "Who were you talking to?"

"You saw him?" I asked, both surprised and relieved.

"Yes, you were talking to an odd-looking man with some kind of device in his hand or something," explained Robbie, "You looked uneasy, so I thought I would come see if you were okay."

Dr. Swagler

I looked around the large hall. Inevitably, I spotted him, as he spotted me at the same time. Dr. Swagler was in the far corner of the large hall, as if he had slithered away without my noticing. He was glaring at me with those devilish eyes. As I glared back at him, I spoke to Robbie.

"Robbie," I began, "the man's name is Dr. Swagler. He says he can speak to the Shadow Orbs."

"Speak with them?" asked Robbie.

"Yes, through soundwaves. Robbie, we have to start investigating a new treatment right away—one that involves sound," I said.

Robbie snapped his fingers.

"My uncle Martin owns a music store in Los Angeles. Some of the world's best music minds visit his shop. I bet he can put us in touch with an expert sound engineer. What do you think?" said Robbie.

"Thanks, Robbie," I said. "It would be a great start."

As I said this, my eyes drifted upward across the large hall. Directly above Dr. Swagler, the self-proclaimed Shadow Master, were three new Shadow Orbs hovering around the corner ceiling above him. I could not believe my eyes. Were these my Shadow Orbs or Dr. Swagler's? After all my treatments, and all the memory juice I had consumed, right before my eyes was this symbol of dread. My legs trembled and my face showed my discontent.

Looking back, I still can't fathom the truth. My fate has been sealed, and I wonder what my dark future will look like. The truth of my fate is this:

The Shadow Orbs are still out there …

Sincerely Yours,

Katerina Chen

THE END

Made in United States
Orlando, FL
15 November 2024

53936470R00059